Outside the Window

by **ANNA EGAN SMUCKER**

illustrated by **STACEY SCHUETT**

ALFRED A. KNOPF · NEW YORK

THIS IS A BORZOI BOOK PUBLISHED BY ALFRED A. KNOPF, INC.

Text copyright © 1994 by Anna Egan Smucker
Illustrations copyright © 1994 by Stacey Schuett
All rights reserved under International and Pan-American Copyright Conventions. Published in the
United States of America by Alfred A. Knopf, Inc., New York, and simultaneously in Canada by
Random House of Canada Limited, Toronto. Distributed by Random House, Inc., New York.

Library of Congress Cataloging-in-Publication Data
Smucker, Anna Egan.
Outside the window / by Anna Egan Smucker ; illustrated by Stacey Schuett.
p.   cm.
Summary: A mother bird describes the bedtime activities of a little boy to her five curious babies.
ISBN 0-679-84023-0 (trade)   ISBN 0-679-94023-5 (lib. bdg.)
[1. Bedtime—Fiction. 2. Birds—Fiction.]   I. Schuett, Stacey, ill.   II. Title.
PZ7.S66478Ou 1994
[E]—dc20   92-33452

Manufactured in the United States of America
10 9 8 7 6 5 4 3 2 1

For Kara, Emily, and Stephanie
　　　—A. E. S.

For Erika Kay, with love
　　　—S. S.

On a strong leafy branch outside the bedroom window of a little boy, there is a nest. In that nest live a mother bird and her five baby birds. The biggest one loves to eat. The medium-sized one loves to play. The cleanest one loves to take baths. The chirpiest one loves to hear stories. And the tiniest one is always sleepy. But they are all very curious about the little boy who lives in the house that their nest in the maple tree can almost touch.

In the evening, when the air cools and the sky turns pink, Mother Bird tucks her babies safely down into their nest. The nest sways gently back and forth in the green-leaved maple tree. And every evening, from the darkness of the nest, the baby birds ask their mother questions about what the little boy is doing.

"Is he asleep yet?" asks the little bird who is always sleepy—and who is almost asleep already.

"No, not yet," says Mother Bird. "He is still playing outside."

"Playing? . . . Still?" asks the little bird who loves to play. "What is he playing?"

"He is making sand pies in his sandbox," says Mother Bird.

"Sand pies? Does the boy eat the sand pies?" asks the little bird who is always hungry.

"No, little one," says Mother Bird. "He doesn't eat the sand pies. He likes juicier things than that."

"Yum," says the hungry little bird. And he imagines the little boy eating a juicy bedtime snack.

"Do I hear water running?" asks the little bird who loves to bathe.

"Yes," says Mother Bird. "The boy is taking his bath."

"Ooh," says the little bird, shivering under his downy feathers. And he imagines the little boy splashing in cool water.

"Is he asleep yet?" asks the sleepy little bird, very sleepily.

"No, not yet," says Mother Bird. "He is brushing his teeth."

"What are 'teeth'?" ask the other baby birds.

"They are big white things inside his beak," says Mother Bird.

"Oh," the baby birds say, wishing they had teeth in their beaks.

"Is he asleep yet?" asks the sleepy little bird, with his eyes closed.

"No, not yet," says Mother Bird. "But he is climbing into his bed now."

"*Mmm,*" says the sleepy little bird, imagining the boy snuggling down in his nest.

"Is it time for the story?" asks the little bird who loves stories.

"Yes, it is time for the story," says Mother Bird. "The boy's mother is opening the book."

"What is the story about?" asks the little bird who loves stories.

"It's about a mother bird and her baby birds," says Mother Bird.

"Oh," says the little bird, and imagines a story all about herself.

"Is the boy asleep yet?" asks the sleepy little bird, in a voice so soft his mother can hardly hear it.

"No, not yet," says Mother Bird. "He is saying his prayers."

"How does he say his prayers?" ask the other baby birds.

"He looks out the window at us and at the stars," says Mother Bird.

"Oh," the little birds say, feeling very important and lifting their heads to try to see the stars too.

"Is the boy asleep . . . yet?" asks the sleepy little bird, too tired to raise his head.

"Almost," says Mother Bird. "His mother is tucking him in and kissing him good night."

"*Mmm,*" the little birds say, snuggling closer together in their dark, warm nest.

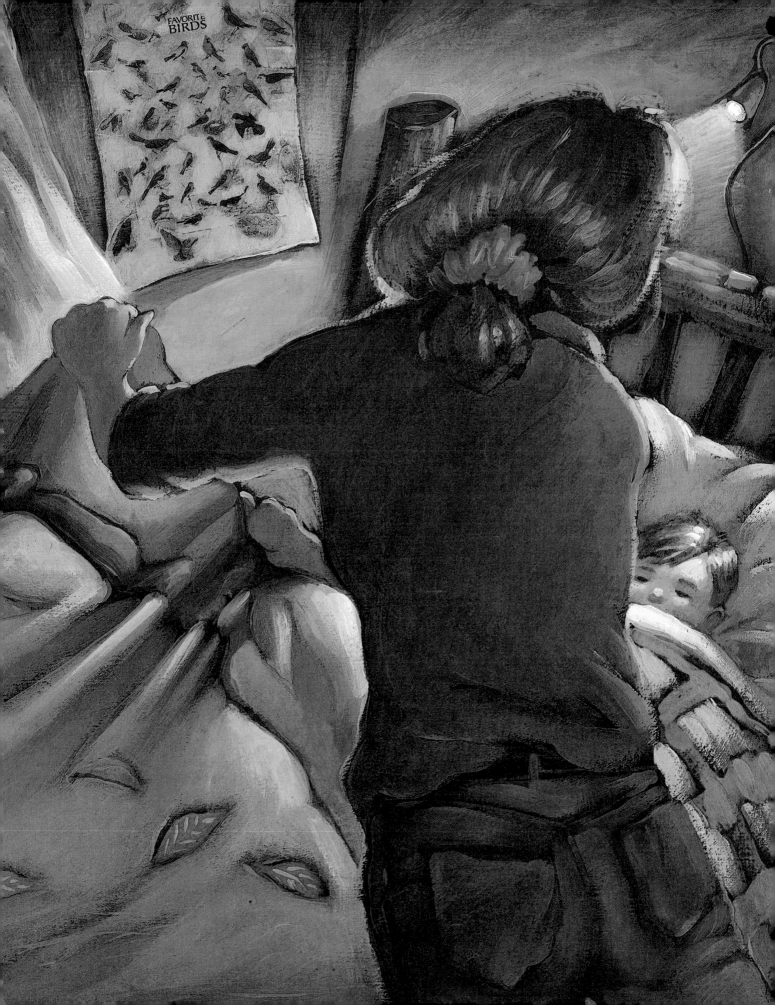

"Is . . . the boy . . . asleep . . . yet?" ask all the little birds, yawning.

"Yes, the boy is asleep now," says Mother Bird.

"Ah," the little birds say and close their sleepy eyes.

"Good night, sweet dreams," says Mother Bird. And
she spreads her soft wings over the baby birds and over the
round bowl of their nest that rocks in the strong arms of
the maple tree—outside the window of the sleeping boy.